MR. HAPPY

by Roger Hargreaves

On the other side of the world, where the sun shines hotter than here, and where the trees are a hundred feet tall, there is a country called Happyland.

As you might very well expect everybody who lives in Happyland is as happy as the day is long. Wherever you go you see smiling faces all round. It's such a happy place that even the flowers seem to smile in Happyland.

And, as well as all the people being happy, all the animals in Happyland are happy as well.

If you've never seen a mouse smile, or a cat, or a dog, or even a worm – go to Happyland!

This is a story about someone who lived there who happened to be called Mr Happy.

Mr Happy was fat and round, and happy!

He lived in a small cottage beside a lake at the foot of a mountain and close to a wood in Happyland.

One day, while Mr Happy was out walking through the tall trees in those woods near his home, he came across something which was really rather extraordinary.

There in the trunk of one of the very tall trees was a door.

Not a very large door, but nevertheless a door. Certainly a door. A small, narrow, yellow door.

Definitely a door!

"I wonder who lives here?" thought Mr Happy to himself, and he turned the handle of that small, narrow, yellow door.

The door wasn't locked and it swung open quite easily.

Just inside the small, narrow, yellow door was a small, narrow, winding staircase, leading downwards.

Mr Happy squeezed his rather large body through the rather thin doorway and began to walk down the stairs.

The stairs went round and round and down and down and round and down and down and round.

Eventually, after a long time, Mr Happy reached the bottom of the staircase.

He looked around and saw, there in front of him, another small, narrow door. But this one was red.

Mr Happy knocked at the door.

"Who's there?" said a voice. A sad, squeaky sort of voice. "Who's there?"

Mr Happy pushed open the red door slowly, and there, sitting on a stool, was somebody who looked exactly like Mr Happy, except that he didn't look happy at all.

In fact he looked downright miserable.

"Hello," said Mr Happy. "I'm Mr Happy."

"Oh, are you indeed," sniffed the person who looked like Mr Happy but wasn't. "Well, my name is Mr Miserable, and I'm the most miserable person in the world."

"Why are you so miserable?" asked Mr Happy.

"Because I am," replied Mr Miserable.

"How would you like to be happy like me?" asked Mr Happy.

"I'd give anything to be happy," said Mr Miserable. "But I'm so miserable I don't think I could ever be happy," he added miserably.

Mr Happy made up his mind quickly. "Follow me," he said.

"Where to?" asked Mr Miserable.

"Don't argue," said Mr Happy, and he went out through the small, narrow, red door.

Mr Miserable hesitated, and then followed.

Up and up the winding staircase they went. Up and up and round and round and up and round and round and up until they came out into the wood.

"Follow me," said Mr Happy again, and they both set off through the wood back to Mr Happy's cottage.

Mr Miserable stayed in Mr Happy's cottage for quite some time. And during that time the most remarkable thing happened.

Because he was living in Happyland Mr Miserable ever so slowly stopped being miserable and started to be happy.

His mouth stopped turning down at the corners.

And ever so slowly it started turning up at the corners.

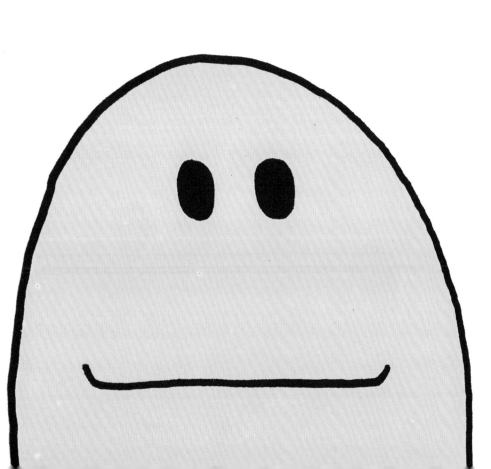

And eventually Mr Miserable did something that he'd never done in the whole of his life.

He smiled!

And then he chuckled, which turned into a giggle, which became a laugh. A big booming hearty huge giant large enormous laugh.

And Mr Happy was so surprised that he started to laugh as well. And both of them laughed and laughed.

They laughed until their sides hurt and their eyes watered.

Mr Miserable and Mr Happy laughed and laughed and laughed and laughed.

They went outside and still they laughed.

And because they were laughing so much everybody who saw them started laughing as well. Even the birds in the trees started to laugh at the thought of somebody called Mr Miserable who just couldn't stop laughing.

And that's really the end of the story except to say that if you ever feel as miserable as Mr Miserable used to you know exactly what to do, don't you?

Just turn your mouth up at the corners.

Go on!

3 Great Offers For Mr Men Fans

1 Token EGMONT WORLD

1 FREE Door Hangers and Posters

In every Mr Men and Little Miss Book like this one you will find a special token. Collect 6 and we will send you either a brilliant Mr. Men or Little Miss poster and a Mr Men or Little Miss double sided, full colour, bedroom door hanger. Apply using the coupon overleaf, enclosing six tokens and a 50p coin for your choice of two items.

Egmont World tokens can be used towards any other Egmont World / World International token scheme promotions., in early learning and story / activity books.

Posters: Tick your preferred choice of either Mr Men ☐ or Little Miss ☐

Door Hangers: Choose from: Mr. Nosey & Mr Muddle ☐, Mr Greedy & Mr Lazy ☐, Mr Tickle & Mr Grumpy ☐, Mr Slow & Mr Busy ☐, Mr Messy & Mr Quiet ☐, Mr Perfect & Mr Forgetful ☐, Little Miss Fun & Little Miss Late ☐, Little Miss Helpful & Little Miss Tidy ☐, Little Miss Busy & Little Miss Brainy ☐, Little Miss Star & Little Miss Fun ☐.
(Please tick)

2 Mr Men Library Boxes

Keep your growing collection of Mr Men and Little Miss books in these superb library boxes. With an integral carrying handle and stay-closed fastener, these full colour, plastic boxes are fantastic. They are just £5.49 each including postage. Order overleaf.

3 Join The Club

To join the fantastic Mr Men & Little Miss Club, check out the page overleaf NOW!

MR MEN and LITTLE MISS™ & © 1998 Mrs. Roger Hargreaves

Join Our Club!

MR·MEN & Little Miss CLUB

When you become a member of the fantastic Mr Men and Little Miss Club you'll receive a personal letter from Mr Happy and Little Miss Giggles, a club badge with your name, and a superb Welcome Pack (pictured below right).

You'll also get birthday and Christmas cards from the Mr Men and Little Misses, 2 newsletters crammed with special offers, privileges and news, and a copy of the 12 page Mr Men catalogue which includes great party ideas.

If it were on sale in the shops, the Welcome Pack alone might cost around £13. But a year's membership is just £9.99 (plus 73p postage) with a 14 day money-back guarantee if you are not delighted!

HOW TO APPLY To apply for any of these three great offers, ask an adult to complete the coupon below and send it with appropriate payment and tokens (where required) to: Mr Men Offers, PO Box 7, Manchester M19 2HD. Credit card orders for Club membership ONLY by telephone, please call: 01403 242727.

To be completed by an adult

❏ **1.** Please send a poster and door hanger as selected overleaf. I enclose six tokens and a 50p coin for post (coin not required if you are also taking up 2. or 3. below).

❏ **2.** Please send __ Mr Men Library case(s) and __ Little Miss Library case(s) at £5.49 each.

❏ **3.** Please enrol the following in the Mr Men & Little Miss Club at £10.72 (inc postage)

Fan's Name:_____ Fan's Address:_____

_____Post Code:_____ Date of birth: __/__/__

Your Name:_____ Your Address:_____

Post Code:_____ Name of parent or guardian (if not you):_____

Total amount due: £_____ (£5.49 per Library Case, £10.72 per Club membership)

❏ I enclose a cheque or postal order payable to Egmont World Limited.

❏ Please charge my MasterCard / Visa account.

Card number: | | | | | | | | | | | | | | | | |

Expiry Date: ____/____   Signature: _____

Data Protection Act: If you do **not** wish to receive other family offers from us or companies we recommend, please tick this box ❏. Offer applies to UK only